# Braids!

## Robert Munsch

illustrated by
## Dave Whamond

Scholastic Canada Ltd.
Toronto  New York  London  Auckland  Sydney
Mexico City  New Delhi  Hong Kong  Buenos Aires

Scholastic Canada Ltd.
604 King Street West, Toronto, Ontario M5V 1E1, Canada

Scholastic Inc.
557 Broadway, New York, NY 10012, USA

Scholastic Australia Pty Limited
PO Box 579, Gosford, NSW 2250, Australia

Scholastic New Zealand Limited
Private Bag 94407, Botany, Manukau 2163, New Zealand

Scholastic Children's Books
Euston House, 24 Eversholt Street, London NW1 1DB, UK

www.scholastic.ca

Library and Archives Canada Cataloguing in Publication
Munsch, Robert N., 1945-, author
Braids! / Robert Munsch ; illustrated by Dave Whamond.
ISBN 978-1-4431-4859-7 (paperback)
I. Whamond, Dave illustrator  II. Title.
PS8576.U575B73 2016       jC813'.54       C2015-906487-2

6  5  4  3  2  1      Printed in Canada  119    16  17  18  19  20

*To Ashley Allman,*
*Guelph, Ontario.*
*—R.M.*

On Saturday, when Ashley was sitting at the breakfast table, her mother came in and said, "Look at your hair. It's a mess! It needs a few braids."

"A few!" yelled Ashley. "You always put in a million braids and you pull on my hair and it hurts and it takes all day! NO! NO! NO! My hair is OK to just go out and play."

Then Ashley ran around the house screaming *"Ahhhh! Ahhhh! Ahhhh! Ahhhh!"* while her mother tried to catch her.

After they had gone around the house seventeen times, Ashley's mother caught her, sat her on a chair and started to braid her hair.

It took two hours because Ashley's
mom braided her hair
back and forth
and back and forth
and back and forth,
AND
up and down
and up and down
and up and down,
AND
round and round
and round and round
and round and round.

6

When she was done, Ashley
looked in the mirror and said,
 "Oh, look!
 "It's beautiful.
 "It's wonderful.
 "But it took forever!
 "I wish you didn't like to braid
my hair."

Ashley went outside and sat down on the front steps. People came by and said, "Hey, Ashley! Nice hair," and Ashley didn't say anything.

Then Ashley's grandmother came by. She said, "Ashley! What wonderful braids. But why are you so mad?"

"It's that mother of mine!" said Ashley. "She likes to braid my hair and it takes all day. Some kids go to the mall, some kids play games, I just get my hair braided."

"Do you know," said her grandmother, "why your mother likes to braid like that?"

"No," said Ashley.

"She learned it from me," said her grandmother. "When your mom was a little girl I used to braid her hair all the time. It took all day."

13

"How come you don't braid her hair now?" said Ashley.

"Can't catch her," said her grandmother.

"Maybe both of us could catch her!" said Ashley.

"Good idea," said her grandmother.

So they went into the house and Ashley's grandmother said to Ashley's mother, "Look at your hair. It needs some BRAIDS!"

"NO, NO, NO!" yelled Ashley's mom. "I am grown-up now and I have important things to do! NO! NO! NO! NO!"

Ashley's grandmother said, "Now come on, sweet pea, I'm going to braid your hair."

Ashley's mom ran around the house screaming *"Ahhhh! Ahhhh! Ahhhh! Ahhhh!"* while Ashley and her grandmother tried to catch her.

They chased Ashley's mother around the house seventeen times until they finally caught her. Then they sat her in a chair and braided her hair for three hours.

It took three hours because they
braided her hair
    back and forth
        and back and forth
            and back and forth,
AND
   up and down
      and up and down
        and up and down,
AND
   round and round
      and round and round
        and round and round.

When they were done, Ashley's mother looked in the mirror and said,

"Oh, look!

"It's beautiful.

"It's wonderful.

"But it took forever.

"I wish you didn't like to braid my hair."

Then Ashley and her mother sat
out on the front steps. Ashley's teacher
came by and said, "My! What lovely
braids. I wish I had hair like that."

"LET'S GET HER!" said Ashley.

"Get WHO?" said the teacher.

"Get YOU!" said Ashley.
"We're going to braid your
hair and it will take all day!"

23

"*Ahhhhhhhhhhhhhhhhhhhh!*" yelled the teacher. She ran down the street, and Ashley and her mom and her grandmother and all the neighbours ran after her.

They chased the teacher around the block seventeen times until Ashley finally caught her. Then they sat her on a mailbox and braided her hair.

It took six hours because they braided it
    back and forth
        and back and forth
            and back and forth,
AND
    up and down
        and up and down
            and up and down,
AND
    round and round
        and round and round
            and round and round.

When they were done the teacher had a thousand little braids in her hair. She looked sort of like a porcupine.

"Looks nice!" said Ashley's grandmother.

"Looks great!" said Ashley's mother.

"Wow!" said Ashley's teacher. "I'm going to wear these braids to school!"

And Ashley decided not to tell her teacher that sometimes people just do not look good in braids.